The White House Mystery

Penn Mullin

High Noon Books
Novato, California

Cover Design and Interior Illustrations: Damon Rarey

International Standard Book Number: 0-87879-959-1

10 09 08 07 06 05
5 4 3 2 1 0 9 8

You'll enjoy all the High Noon Books. Write for
a free full list of titles.

Contents

1 Hello, Washington! 1

2 High Places 5

3 A Great Man 9

4 The President's House 16

5 Famous Rooms 22

6 Missing! 26

7 The Closed-Off Rooms 31

8 In Lincoln's Room 37

9 Lisa's Secret 40

All aboard! Juan; Mike, their van driver; Justin; Miss Lake, their teacher; Amy; and Lisa smile for the camera before taking off on their trip.

When Miss Lake's seventh grade class entered the President's *See America the Beautiful* contest, they didn't think they had a chance to win. It was fun thinking they might, so everyone wrote and sent in a short essay on "What Do You Like Best About Being an American?"

They could hardly believe it when the letter came. It said: "The essays sent in by four members of your class were outstanding. These students have won a three-week trip across the United States with their teacher. All expenses will be paid."

The class clapped when Miss Lake finished reading the letter and Lisa, Amy, Justin, and Juan went home to pack their bags.

CHAPTER 1

Hello, Washington!

Mike stopped the van in front of a tall white pointed tower.

"Wow! How tall is that?" Justin asked.

"It is 555 feet high," Mike said. "The Washington Monument is the highest stone building in the world."

"It's named for George Washington, our first President. This city is named for him, too," said Miss Lake, their teacher and leader on the trip.

"I'm sure glad we're here," Lisa said.

"It was a long ride in the van," said Justin.

"Can we go clear to the top?" Amy asked.

"Yes. There's an elevator. Let's go get in line," Miss Lake told the kids.

Everybody said goodbye to Mike. It felt good to get off the van. They had been riding all day.

"Look!" Lisa said. She pointed to a ring of flags. The flags were all around the monument.

"There are fifty of them. One for each state in our United States," Miss Lake said. "Follow me."

She and the kids lined up for the elevator.

"How old is the Washington Monument?"

2

Justin wanted to know.

"It was started in 1848," Miss Lake said. "But money ran out. They had to stop building. It wasn't finished until 1884."

"That must have looked funny. Half a tower sitting there," Juan laughed.

"Look, there's the Capitol down there." Miss Lake pointed to a large building. It had a high round top. It was at the far end of a long green lawn.

"Can we go in the Capitol building, too?" Juan asked.

"Yes. The Capitol has two parts. We will see them both. They are the House and the Senate. Many of our country's laws are made there," said Miss Lake.

Lisa was looking up at the tower. "I sometimes get sick in high places," she said.

"Just don't look down, Lisa," Amy said.

"And don't stand near me," Juan laughed.

CHAPTER 2

High Places

"Look. Here's the elevator. Let's get in," Justin said.

The elevator went up fast. The kids watched Lisa. She didn't look sick—yet.

Then they were at the top. Everybody got out of the elevator. There were windows all around them.

"Look how far you can see!" Justin said.

"I see the White House," Amy said.

"And there's the Lincoln Memorial, too,"

The Washington Monument—
A Famous Landmark

Miss Lake said. "We can walk there next."

Lisa stayed away from the windows. "I can see fine standing back here," she said.

"What's that building?" Justin asked Miss Lake.

"The one with the round top? That's the Jefferson Memorial," she said. "It is named for Thomas Jefferson. He wrote the Declaration of Independence in 1776. He also was President of our country later on."

"Washington is a beautiful place," said Amy. "I'm glad we came up here. Now we can see where everything is."

"Juan, do you feel OK? You look a little sick," said Miss Lake.

"Stand away from the windows," Amy said.

Juan didn't say anything. He went to stand beside Lisa.

"Let's start down now," Miss Lake said. "We'll see the Lincoln Memorial next. Lisa and Juan, don't worry. No more high places today! I promise."

Lisa and Juan were the first ones to get on the down elevator.

CHAPTER 3

A Great Man

"Why is Abraham Lincoln famous?" Miss Lake asked the kids.

"He freed the slaves," Lisa said. She was glad to be back on the ground.

"That's right. He said that one person cannot own another person. That was in 1865. He was a great President. People wanted to honor him. So they built this beautiful building." Miss Lake pointed to the Lincoln Memorial.

"Four score and seven years ago . . ."

"Is Lincoln buried inside there?" asked Lisa.

"No, he is buried in Springfield, Illinois. That is where he lived before he became President," said Miss Lake.

"Can we go up the stairs now?" Juan asked.

"Yes. Let's go," Miss Lake told the kids.

They all started up the stone stairs.

"I can see his statue inside," Justin said. "It's really big."

They stopped in front of Lincoln's statue. Everybody was quiet. They just looked up at it. The statue was of Lincoln sitting in a chair. He was looking out over the city.

"I bet that statue took a long time to carve," Lisa said.

"It did. Six years," said Miss Lake.

"What kind of stone is it?" Juan asked.

"It is white marble," Miss Lake said.

"Lincoln looks like he was really a kind man," Justin said.

"He almost looks alive," said Amy.

"Come and see this," Miss Lake said. She pointed to words carved into the walls.

"Did Lincoln say these words?" Justin asked.

"Yes. These words are from a speech he gave," Miss Lake said. "They say good things about freedom for all people."

"It's my turn to write the postcard back to school," Juan said. "I want to find one of the Lincoln Memorial."

"Good idea," said Miss Lake.

"Lincoln would be happy today," Juan said. "People have a lot more freedom."

"That's right, Juan. Lincoln helped people to get that freedom. You have heard of Dr. Martin Luther King, Jr. He gave his famous speech right here," Miss Lake said. "I remember. I was here with my parents then."

"Was that speech called 'I have a dream'?" Justin asked.

"Yes," said Miss Lake. "He talked about more freedom for African-Americans. He picked a good place for his speech, didn't he?"

"That's for sure," Juan said.

"I feel like whispering," Amy said. "It's as if Lincoln were really here."

"I feel the same way. Now I want to see Lincoln's bedroom in the White House," said Lisa.

"I don't think it's open," Miss Lake said.

"Why not?" Lisa asked.

"Some rooms are closed. Like the rooms for the President's family," said Miss Lake.

"But I want to see Lincoln's bed!" Lisa looked sad. "I heard it's very big."

"Buy a postcard of it," Justin said.

"Very funny. Who knows? Lincoln's room

might be open today after all!" Lisa smiled a secret smile.

"Come on, kids. There's our van," said Miss Lake.

CHAPTER 4

The President's House

"Is this really the White House? I can't believe I'm here," Amy said. "I'm so glad we are on this trip."

"It sure is. And it's time for our tour," said Miss Lake. "Let's go get in line."

She led the kids off the van. Then they met their guide.

"Good morning," the man said. "I'm Ed Walsh. You can call me Ed. I'm your guide today at the White House. We have a lot to

1600 Pennsylvania Avenue

see. Are you ready?"

"Yes. Will we get to see the President?" Lisa asked.

"No. His part of the White House is not open to visitors," Ed said.

"Who was the first president who lived here?" Juan asked.

"John Adams, in the year 1800," Ed said. "But the White House burned down in 1812. It had to be built again."

Ed took everybody into the White House. First they saw the library. There were many shelves of books on the walls. Ed said there were almost 3,000 books there!

"Is it OK to touch them?" Justin asked.

"No. The books are very old," Ed said. "So are the tables and chairs. They break very easily.

"Do we get to go up there?" Lisa pointed to some large stone stairs.

"Yes, we'll go up to the State Floor now," Ed said. "The President brings guests there. Follow me."

"How many rooms are in the White House?" Miss Lake asked Ed.

"There are 132 rooms. We will see only a few," Ed said.

"Are there really ghosts here?" Juan asked.

"Oh, yes. Some rooms have their very own ghosts," Ed said.

"Really and truly?" Lisa asked.

"Yes. Some people say they saw Lincoln. He was in his Sitting Room," Ed told her.

"Wow," Juan said. "Sounds spooky. I sure wouldn't want to sleep in his room."

"I don't know," Lisa said. "I think it would be neat."

"Even if the ghost came?" Justin asked.

"If it was Lincoln's ghost. That would be OK," Lisa said.

"No way. You would be out of that room so fast," Amy said.

"OK. Don't believe me," Lisa said. "Where else did people see ghosts, Ed?"

"In some of the closed-off rooms. Rooms

that no one goes in much," Ed said.

"Somebody could hide out. They could stay there a long time," Lisa said.

"Don't bet on it," said Justin.

"Remember all the guards," Juan said.

Lisa just smiled.

CHAPTER 5

Famous Rooms

"This is the Green Room. Does anyone know how it got its name?" Ed laughed.

The kids looked into the room. Its walls were a beautiful green color. A low fire burned in the fireplace.

"What is this room used for now, Ed?" Miss Lake asked.

"Small meetings," Ed said. "Look at the beautiful old tables and chairs. This is how the room looked way back in 1800."

"Is the Blue Room next?" Justin asked.

"You are right. Follow me. The President meets here with his guests," Ed said. He led them into the next room.

"The Blue Room is very famous," said Miss Lake. "Many important people come here."

"Like kings and queens?" Amy asked.

"And astronauts and movie stars?" Lisa asked.

"Yes, all of these people and many more," Ed said.

"Just think—they stood right here in this spot," said Lisa.

"This room doesn't look very cozy," Juan

said as he looked around.

"Remember. No one lives down here," Ed said. "The rooms upstairs are cozier."

"Is the Oval Office up there?" Amy asked. "Where the President works?"

"Yes, it is on the second floor," Ed told her.

"I wish we could go up there," Lisa said.

"Dream on," Justin told her.

They followed Ed into the next room.

"Wow! A lot of people could eat in here!" Amy said. She looked into the large white room. There were many paintings on the walls.

Ed said, "You are right. One hundred and forty guests can eat here. This is called the

State Dining Room."

"Does the President eat here every night?" Lisa asked.

"No. Only if he has special guests. Like the Queen of England. Then the table is made much bigger," Ed said.

"I'd love to eat here. Just one night. That's all I'd ask," said Lisa.

"Sorry, Lisa. They don't serve burgers here," Juan laughed.

"Come on, kids. Ed is getting ahead of us." Miss Lake started down a long hall. Everybody followed her. Everybody but one.

CHAPTER 6

Missing!

"We are at the other end of the White House," Ed said. "I'll show you the East Room. It is the largest of all. It is eighty feet long!"

The room was all white and gold. It had a shiny wood floor. There were large paintings on the walls of this room, too.

"Guests come here after dinner," Ed said. "They see shows and listen to music. Or they dance."

"Wow! You could do some cool moves

here!" Juan did a few fast dance steps.

"Think of the party you could have!" Amy said.

Everyone was busy looking at the East Room.

Suddenly Miss Lake said, "Where's Lisa?"

"She's gone!" cried Amy.

"She was here a minute ago," Justin said. "Or was she?"

"I'll call Security," said Ed. He picked up his radio. Then he placed a call. "This is Ed. East Room. We have a missing girl. Age twelve. Black hair. Last seen in State Dining Room."

Juan turned to Amy. "Do you think she

snuck off?" he asked.

"She could have. You know how Lisa is," Amy said.

"Security will find her. Don't worry," Ed told Miss Lake.

"Lisa is very good at hiding." Justin started to laugh.

"But our guards are very good at finding," Ed said.

"Lisa said she wanted to go to the top floor," Amy said.

"She really wants to see the President," said Justin.

"If I know Lisa, she will!" Juan laughed.

"What should we do now, Ed?" asked

Miss Lake. She looked worried.

"We'll go down to the ground floor. We will wait there until they find Lisa," Ed said.

"We might have a long wait, said Amy.

"We'll see. Follow me down the stairs," Ed told them.

"I bet Lisa is in the Oval Office by now," Justin laughed.

"I can't wait to hear what she did," Amy told him.

"I'm worried about Lisa," Miss Lake said.

"Has anybody else been lost in here?" Juan asked Ed.

"Not for long. Our guards are fast," Ed said. "They know every inch of this place."

"I'm scared for Lisa," Amy said. "What if she is lost? What about the ghosts up there?"

"Lisa can take care of herself," Justin said. "I bet she wouldn't run. But the ghosts would!"

Everybody got to the bottom of the stairs.

"You can sit down here by the door," Ed said. "I'll go check about Lisa."

Miss Lake and the kids sat down on a bench.

"I wish I could see what she's doing. I want to know if she's OK," Amy said.

"I hope the guards find her soon," said Miss Lake.

"What happens if they don't?" Juan asked.

Miss Lake did not answer.

CHAPTER 7

The Closed-Off Rooms

Lisa had to hide. Someone would see her. Maybe a guard. She ran down the hall. There was a corner ahead. She ran around it. There was no one there. Safe—for now!

She was on the second floor of the White House! This was where the President lived! And where Lincoln's bedroom was! And no one had stopped her yet!

Lisa didn't have much time. Miss Lake would soon see that she was gone. Then Ed would know. Ed would tell the guards. She would get caught. But first she had something to do. She had to see Lincoln's bedroom. It must be close by.

She saw a door. Maybe this was it. Would it be locked? She tried it. The heavy door opened!

Should she go in? Were there guards inside? Lisa slowly walked into the room. There was no one there. She was all alone. Lincoln's bedroom. She was really here. She looked around her.

The walls were yellow. There were lots of old tables and chairs. And the biggest bed she had ever seen! Lisa went closer. She wanted to touch it. The wood was a red-brown color. The part behind the pillows looked ten feet high! Lisa felt very small. She touched the soft white bedspread.

Suddenly she heard voices. They were in the hall. Were they looking for her? She must hide. But where? She saw another door. Maybe it was a closet. She ran and opened it. No. It was another room.

The room was empty. No one was in it. Lisa went in. Was there a place to hide? She saw a door. Was it a closet or another room? She heard voices again. They were coming in! Lisa opened the door. It was a closet. Quickly she went inside and hid.

She was just in time. Someone came into the room.

"I know I heard something," a voice said.

"The ghost I bet," someone said. "It likes this room best."

"No. Ghosts don't make noise. I know I heard something. Maybe it's the missing girl."

"OK. We better check the room out. Just to make sure."

Lisa was scared. She was scared of the ghosts. And she was scared the guards would find her. Then she would have to leave. And she wasn't ready to do that yet. She needed just a little more time.

Could she hide in the closet? It was very

dark. Lisa felt some big boxes on the floor. She hid behind them. Would the guards see her?

She heard footsteps coming close! They stopped. Lisa's heart pounded. The door slowly opened. Light came in. Lisa didn't move.

"Nobody here," the guard said. The door closed. It was dark again in the closet. Lisa couldn't believe it. They hadn't seen her!

"Well, I'm glad we checked. I guess the girl is downstairs by now. Let's go find out."

"OK. We'll leave the Lincoln Sitting Room to the ghosts."

"Good idea. Did you hear about the President's dog? He will never come into this room. He just stands outside the door and barks."

"He knows there's a ghost in here," the guard said.

"That's right. Animals always know."

"Let's go downstairs."

"OK with me."

Lisa heard the footsteps going away.

CHAPTER 8

In Lincoln's Room

Lisa stayed in the closet. Were the guards gone? She had to be sure. Then she opened the door. She was safe!

She looked around the room. So this was Lincoln's Sitting Room. She saw a small desk. Was this where Lincoln wrote his great speeches? Is this the room where he came to be alone? The room had a special feeling about it. Lisa was glad she had found it. She walked over to the desk.

Suddenly she had a funny feeling. She knew someone else was in the room. But the door had not opened. She turned around quickly. Then she saw him. Just a flash of him. A tall, dark-haired man in a black suit. Then he was gone. Right through the wall.

Lisa didn't move. It was Lincoln. She was sure of it. Lincoln's ghost. She had really seen him. Would anyone believe her? The kids would say she had just made it up. But she knew this was real.

Lisa wanted to go tell everybody. It was OK if she got caught now. That didn't seem to matter. She opened the door slowly.

The hall was empty. She started off to the

stairs. She was still shaking. Lincoln's ghost! Where was he going? Did he live in the Sitting Room? Who else had ever seen him? Lisa's head was full of questions.

Suddenly she heard voices! They were coming around the corner. Lisa stopped and stood still. She was sure it was the guards. They came around the corner. Lots of tall men in suits. Walking fast. They came closer. Lisa still didn't move. They were coming right at her!

Then the men turned. They went into a room. But they looked at her first. She got a good look at their faces. One face she knew. It was the President.

CHAPTER 9

Lisa's Secret

Lisa couldn't believe it. She had seen the President! The President of the United States. And he had been only fifteen feet away!

"Here you are! We've been looking all over for you," a voice said.

"Oh! You have?" Lisa jumped. She hadn't seen the man.

"Yes. You are missing from your group," the man said. "Everyone has been worried about you."

"I'm sorry. I really am. I'll go down now," Lisa said.

"OK. Your teacher is waiting for you. Your name is Lisa?" the man asked.

"Yes," said Lisa. "Was that really the President I just saw?"

"It sure was. He was going to the Oval Office. I'm in the President's Secret Service. My name is Bill," the man said.

The Secret Service! Lisa was scared. Now she was really in trouble. What did they do to people who hid in the White House?

"Where were you, Lisa? The guards looked everywhere," Bill said.

"I was in two places," Lisa said.

41

"Where?" Bill asked.

"The Lincoln Bedroom first. Then his Sitting Room," Lisa said.

"But they checked there," Bill told her.

Lisa said nothing. They started down the stairs.

Everybody was waiting for her.

"Here she is," Bill said.

"Lisa! You're found! You had us so scared," said Miss. Lake.

"I'm really sorry," Lisa said. "I guess I did a stupid thing."

Then everybody began talking. They stood all around Lisa. They had lots of questions. But Miss Lake spoke first.

"Lisa, don't ever go off alone like that," she said. "Rules are made to keep you safe."

"I know it was wrong," said Lisa.

"Where did you go? And why?" Ed asked.

"I went up to the second floor. I wanted to see Lincoln's bed. And maybe the President," said Lisa.

"Fat chance of that," Justin laughed.

"Well, some funny things happened," Lisa said.

"What kinds of things?" Amy asked.

"You saw the President," Juan laughed.

"You saw the ghosts?" Justin asked.

"Maybe yes and maybe no." Lisa smiled. She didn't want to tell it all just yet. It was such a wonderful secret. And right now it belonged just to her.

"Now for our last stop of the day," said Mike. "We are going to walk over to the Elipse. It's very close."

"What's the Elipse?" asked Justin.

"It is a large round park which is the zero milestone for measuring all distances from Washington. Just think. Our route to our next stop, New York, will start at the Elipse."

"New York—I'm ready!" said Lisa.

"Whoa, Lisa," laughed Miss Lake. "Haven't you had enough excitement for one day?"